In the year 776 BC the first
Olympic Games were held in a town
called Olympia in Ancient Greece.
Many years later, a boy named Olly
grew up there
an Olympic
he would have to be better than his
arch-enemy, Spiro…

ORCHARD BOOKS
338 Euston Road, London NW1 3BH
Orchard Books Australia
Level 17/207 Kent Street, Sydney, NSW 2000

First published in 2011
First paperback publication in 2012

ISBN 978 1 40831 182 0 (hardback)
ISBN 978 1 40831 190 5 (paperback)

Text and illustrations © Shoo Rayner 2011

The right of Shoo Rayner to be identified as the author and
illustrator of this work has been asserted by him in accordance
with the Copyright, Designs and Patents Act, 1988.

A CIP catalogue record for this book is available
from the British Library.

1 3 5 7 9 10 8 6 4 2 (hardback)
1 3 5 7 9 10 8 6 4 2 (paperback)

Printed in Great Britain

Orchard Books is a division of Hachette Children's Books,
an Hachette UK company.
www.hachette.co.uk

THROW FOR GOLD

SHOO RAYNER

ORCHARD

CHAPTER ONE

"Not like that, Olly!" Eury sighed. Eury was the greatest discus thrower in Olympia. He was teaching Olly some skills. "You're trying too hard," Eury explained. "Just relax and let the discus fly, like this."

Olly's arch-enemy, Spiro, smirked. "*I'll* show you how it's done." He picked up a stone discus and swung it round his body a couple of times. Then, grunting and groaning like a grumpy old pig, he hurled the discus into the air.

Spiro's dog, Kerberos, chased after it, yapping and barking wildly. He'd learned the hard way that it hurt to catch a heavy discus in the air, but he still liked trying to kill them once they were safely on the ground!

Olly's dad, Ariston, ran the gymnasium in Olympia, the town where the Olympic Games were held every four years. Olly and Spiro worked there, helping the best athletes in the world while they trained.

Olly dreamed of being an Olympic champion one day, so he had been thrilled when Eury had offered to give the boys some private coaching.

"Hmm!" Eury sighed, as Spiro went to rescue his discus from Kerberos. "Brute force is one way to throw a discus, Spiro, but you don't have a lot of style!"

Eury was tall, with a mass of blonde curls that he tied back with a strip of leather. His shoulders bulged with muscles that he'd built up over his career as a discus thrower.

"Ha!" Spiro laughed. "Who needs style? I'll always throw a discus further than Olly. He's just a little weed!"

Olly ignored him. He'd been putting up with Spiro for most of his life. Spiro was bigger than him and a year older. Spiro beat him at everything, but Olly was determined that things were going to change.

Eury turned to Olly. "When I first became a champion, Euros, the east wind, was blowing gently," he explained. "I called on the wind to help my discus fly, and it did. No one had ever thrown as far before. You need strength like Spiro, but you need something else too…I call it the spirit of the wind."

"Ahh!" Olly exclaimed. "So that's why you're called Eury?"

Eury smiled. "I've trusted Euros to help me ever since."

"Ha!" Spiro laughed. "What a load of superstitious rubbish! I'll *always* throw further than Olly because I'm bigger and stronger than him, and I *always* will be." Spiro picked up an armful of discuses and marched back to the changing rooms. He didn't need any more advice. He knew everything he needed to know already! Kerberos trotted behind him, hoping his master might drop a discus so he could kill it.

"Try again, Olly," Eury suggested.
He was a very patient teacher. "Don't
think about strength or technique,
just imagine you are the discus, flying
through the air, lifted by the wind."

Olly chose a discus, felt its weight and swung it round, twisting his body at the hips. He tried to imagine that he was going to fly with the discus, further than Spiro had ever thrown before.

Olly wound himself up like a spring. As he spun round, a warm breeze picked up and a spiral of dust twisted across the practice area. Olly let go of the discus and followed it with his gaze.

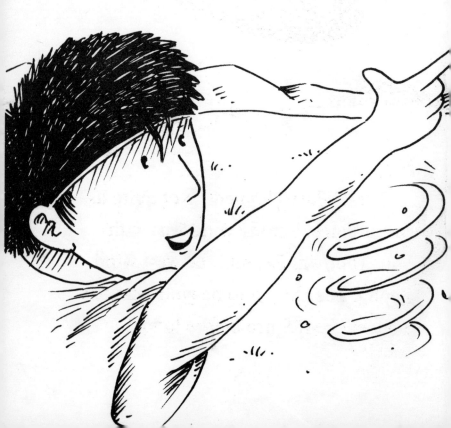

The discus seemed to hover forever, before it began slowly arcing down towards the ground.

"Yes!" Eury clapped. "Not quite as far as Spiro, but the wind was with you. That was Zephyr, the west wind. Zephyr has chosen to be your partner. You will beat Spiro before long!"

Olly was amazed. He knew he hadn't thrown the discus as hard as before, yet the throw had been completely different, almost as if... Was Eury right? Had Zephyr really chosen to help him?

Olly and Eury picked up the rest of the discuses and walked back to the changing rooms. It was nearly lunchtime, and one of Olly's jobs was to lay the tables for the athletes.

"Just keep practising, Olly," Eury called after him. "Throw that discus over and over again. And always remember that Zephyr has chosen you: let the wind take your discus and let it fly."

"Thanks, Eury!" Olly yelled. Although he saw Eury every day, he was still a bit starstruck. After all, Eury was an Olympic champion!

CHAPTER TWO

Olly was hungry after his work-out,
but he wasn't allowed to eat until he
and Spiro had finished serving the
athletes their lunch.

In the large, cool dining hall, Olly
laid out bread, cheese and salad on
the long wooden tables. The athletes
tumbled into the hall in high spirits,
calling to one another, laughing
and joking.

Simonedes, their old, wrinkled history teacher, stood up and cleared his throat. The room hushed. Everyone loved hearing Simonedes' stories about the gods and the heroes of ancient times.

Olly didn't mind waiting for his food. This was his favourite part of the day.

Often, Olly would forget where he was while Simonedes told his tales. He would imagine he was Icarus, flying too close to the sun...

...or Theseus, slaying the bull-headed Minotaur.

"Today," Simonedes began,
"I shall tell you the tale of Acrisius,
who was once the king of Argos.
A propehesy said that Acrisius would
die a violent death at the hands of
his grandson. Eventually, Acrisius's
daughter had a son, whose father was
Zeus, the greatest of the gods. The
child was named Perseus."

"Perseus!" roared the athletes, raising their cups in salute. Perseus was one of their favourite heroes.

Olly looked up at the paintings on the walls and imagined he was Perseus, slayer of the snake-headed Gorgon.

Simonedes' voice was quiet but forceful. His audience listened with rapt attention. "Acrisius loved his daughter and couldn't bring himself to kill her, or his grandson, with his own hands. But to try and save his own life, he set them adrift at sea in an old wooden chest, thinking they would drown and be eaten by the fishes.

"But Zeus saw all this and watched over his son. He guided the child and his mother safely to the island of Seriphos, where Perseus grew up to be the hero we all know and love.

"Many years later, Perseus joined in the games at Larissa. When it was his turn to throw the discus, Perseus tripped. The discus slipped from his hand and flew towards the crowd of spectators…"

The room fell silent as Simonedes came to the high point of the story.

"Little did Perseus know, but his grandfather, Acrisius, was watching the games. The discus sliced through the air like an arrow seeking a target. It hit Acrisius and killed him instantly. The prophecy had come true!"

The athletes remained hushed as Simonedes rolled up his scroll and shuffled between the tables on his way back to the library.

The silence was broken by an athlete called Kimon, who spoke in a slow, drawling voice. "Hey, Olly! We've run out of bread on this table!"

Olly shook himself out of his daydream. But before he could move, Eury stood up and began tossing loaves of flat bread from his table towards Kimon.

"Catch them, Kimon!" Eury laughed.

The loaves spun through the air, floating gracefully across the dining room, as if they knew exactly where they were going.

As Kimon stretched and caught the loaves, the rest of the athletes counted loudly: "One!

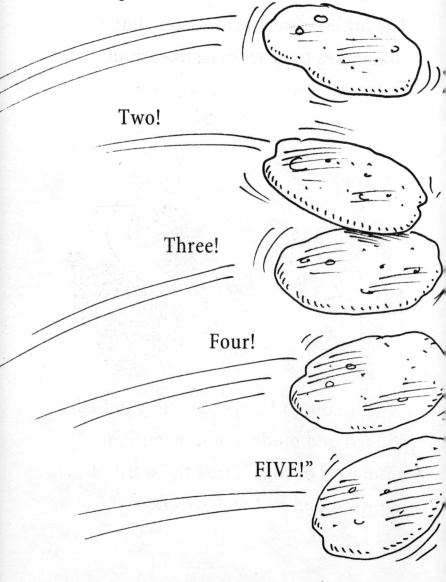

Two!

Three!

Four!

FIVE!"

Kimon held the last loaf above his head like a trophy. The dining hall erupted in whistles and cheers. The athletes were grown men, but sometimes they behaved like small children!

Olly caught Eury's eye. Eury smiled, winked and made a motion with his hand as if to say, "Trust the spirit of the wind and let the discus fly!"

CHAPTER THREE

Olly and Spiro cleared up the dining hall and went to the kitchen to eat their own meal. Olly's sister, Chloe, joined them. Kerberos sat under the table.

Olly bit a mouthful of his bread, which was stuffed with cheese and salad. Olive oil dribbled down his chin. He couldn't get the image of Eury's flying bread out of his mind. An idea was rolling around his head.

"Is it possible to make a loaf of bread the same size as a discus?" he wondered aloud.

"How would I know?" Spiro snarled. "I just eat the stuff!"

Kerberos growled and wagged his tail, as if to say, "Me too!"

Chloe gave Kerberos a piece of
her bread. No wonder he loved her
so much! "Why don't you ask Nestor?"
she suggested.

"Nestor!" Olly shouted towards
the dark end of the kitchen. "Can you
make bread that looks like a discus?"

Nestor – the huge, round, jovial cook – loomed out of the shadows. He threw his arms wide and squeezed Olly until he thought he might burst.

"Olly! Olly! Olly!" Nestor boomed. "I always knew there was more to you than sport. Come! Nestor will teach you the secrets of making bread. It is hard work, but anything of worth is hard work!"

"Hard work!" Spiro groaned.
"I don't like the sound of that!" He
wrapped the rest of his food in a cloth
and left. Kerberos followed, his claws
clicking on the stone floor.

Olly threw some wood into the oven,
while Nestor and Chloe got everything
ready to make the dough for the bread.

"By the time the dough is ready," Nestor explained, "the oven will be just the right temperature to cook it."

To make the dough, Nestor showed Olly and Chloe how to measure flour into a bowl. Next, he poured in a cloudy liquid that smelled like vinegar.

"This liquid is the magic ingredient – grape juice!" Nestor exclaimed. "It contains yeast, you see."

"What's magic about yeast?" Chloe whispered.

"Yeast gives life to the bread. It makes it rise!" Nestor said, waving his hands in the air.

They mixed the liquid into the flour.

Next, Olly and Chloe rolled and kneaded the dough.

"Now we leave the dough in the warming oven to rise, and let the yeast do its magic," said Nestor.

CHAPTER FOUR

It was hot in the kitchen, but it was even hotter outside, where the midsummer sun blazed down on the sizzling pavements of Olympia. Most sensible people went to bed and slept for the afternoon, until the air cooled down a bit.

But Olly was far too excited to sleep – he wanted to see how his bread would come out! So he and Chloe spent the afternoon helping Nestor prepare the food for the evening meal. They chopped…and mixed…and wrapped things in vine leaves…

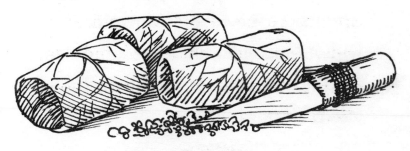

…and occasionally dipped their fingers in the honey pot, just to check that it was still sweet enough!

"How wonderful to have such willing students of the culinary arts!" Nestor sighed, wiping a tear from the corner of his eye as he peeled and chopped an onion. "Everyone in Olympia is obsessed with sport! Ha! You can't live on sport, you know! And where would all the athletes be without my good food, eh?"

Olly and Chloe smiled at each other. Nestor always made a lot of fuss about cooking!

After an hour or so the dough had gently risen and was twice the size it had been before.

Nestor showed Olly and Chloe how to knead the bread even more – bashing it...

and folding it...

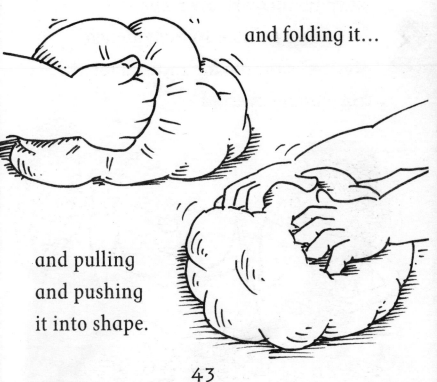

and pulling and pushing it into shape.

Nestor cut the lump of dough into four pieces, and they moulded each one into the shapes and size of discuses.

"This is my baker's shovel," Nestor said, holding a long-handled tool that looked like a flat, square-ended spade. He gave it to Olly and showed him how to scoop the bread onto it.

"Slide the dough into the oven," Nestor said. "Do it slowly. Show the bread some respect."

A short while later, as the kitchen filled with the wonderful aroma of fresh bread, Chloe used the shovel to flip the loaves over so they would cook evenly on both sides.

Finally, Olly scooped the finished loaves out of the oven and slipped them onto the table.

"Fabulous!" Nestor enthused. "You two are going to make great cooks. Now, what are you going to eat with your marvellous bread? Honey and yogurt? Cheese? Olives? Tomatoes? Or are they special loaves to be sacrificed and eaten by the gods?"

"They're not for eating!" Olly said. "They're for discus practice!"

Nestor's eyes nearly popped out of his head. His jaw dropped and his mouth opened in disbelief. "Sport!" he wailed, throwing his hands in the air. "It's all anyone thinks of in this crazy town...sport!"

CHAPTER FIVE

"When I practise throwing the discus my arms get so tired," Olly explained to Chloe. "I saw Eury throw some bread across the dining room, and I had a brainwave: I could practise my technique without having to pick up heavy discuses all the time."

"It's a great idea!" Chloe smiled. "Let's see if it works."

They stood in the shade of a large acacia tree. It was a little cooler outside now and the air was filled with the loud chirruping of cicadas, the noisy insects that infested the trees.

Olly handled one of the loaves and practised his wrist action a couple of times, before letting it go. The loaf spun round and round and floated across the courtyard a couple of metres off the ground. Olly was mesmerised. It seemed to fly forever.

The round loaf lifted slightly, came to a halt in midair and then gently dropped to the ground.

"Wow!" Chloe yelled. "I want a go!"
Chloe loved sport as much as Olly, even
though she would never be allowed to
compete as an athlete in Olympia.

She ran across the courtyard and
picked up the loaf. Copying what Olly
had done, she threw it back to him.

Again the loaf spun and flew threw
the air. As Olly ran towards it, the loaf
appeared to drop gently into his hands.

"That's amazing!" Olly laughed.
"Here, see if you can catch it."

They threw the bread back and
forth, laughing and leaping, running
around after their new flying invention.

But bread was not the best material
to make a discus out of. Before long,
the first loaf had become damaged
around the edges. It flew off-course
and crash-landed every time.

Great big chunks fell off and soon
the loaf was reduced to crumbs. A flock
of sparrows flew down from the tree
and ate up the mess!

"We're not finished yet," Olly said, picking up the next loaf. "One down, three to go."

As he practised, Olly watched how the bread spun and flew, learning how to work with the spirit of the wind.

Just as the third loaf was getting a bit crumbly, Spiro and Kerberos appeared in the courtyard and grabbed it.

"Let's have a go!" Spiro growled. He flung the bread with all his might. It sailed up into the tree and stuck fast in its branches. The sparrows set to work on it straight away.

"Be gentle!" Olly said. "This is how you do it." He took the last loaf and sent it skimming across the courtyard.

But Kerberos had seen the sparrows eating the bread and had realised that this was not a normal discus. He gave chase, yapping and barking as he leaped into the air and caught the spinning loaf in his slavering jaws. He shook it to make sure it was dead, then swallowed it down in three mighty mouthfuls.

"All our hard work gone to waste," Olly sighed. "That's the end of that game!"

"Good boy, Kerberos!" Spiro smirked. "Well caught." He turned to go. "See you at discus practice tomorrow," Spiro taunted over his shoulder.

CHAPTER SIX

꽈꽈꽈꽈꽈꽈꽈꽈꽈꽈꽈꽈

"That's a good throw, Spiro," laughed Eury, the next day. "You still have no style or technique, but you do have brute strength!"

"And that's just what Olly doesn't have," Spiro grinned. "Olly's a weakling. Always has been, and always will be."

Olly ignored him. Spiro's taunts often made him angry, but now he felt quite calm.

He had Zephyr the west wind on his side and his mind was tuned in to the way a discus flew.

Olly picked up a discus and felt its weight in his hand. He twisted his body at the hips and let the discus fly into the air. It was clear straight away that it was a great throw, and Spiro knew it. There was no way he was going to let Olly beat him.

"Kerberos," he snapped, pointing at the discus. "Kill!"

Kerberos leaped into action. Hoping it was another one of Olly's tasty flying loaves, he chased after the discus as fast as he could.

The discus gently arced towards the ground. Kerberos threw himself into the air and snapped his teeth around the heavy stone, then immediately fell to the ground, whining and whimpering. The discus landed just short of Spiro's throw.

"There you are!" Spiro said. "I'm still the best." He turned on his heel and stormed off. Kerberos followed, limping slightly.

Eury winked at Olly. "Come on, try again."

CHAPTER SEVEN

Olly took his time. He chose another
discus and studied its surface. He
could see the shapes of ancient
fossilised creatures embedded in the
stone. The discus seemed to have its
own animal spirit.

Olly swung his arm, twisting his
body at the hips, building up speed
and momentum. His arm
curved gracefully. He
didn't throw the discus
– instead, he just let it
go, trusting in Zephyr,
the west wind, to carry
it through the air.

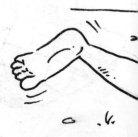

Olly never took his eye off the discus. He followed its flight through the air, where it seemed to hang, suspended, as if held up by the wind itself.

Slowly, almost as if someone had put a brake on time, the discus sloped gently downwards and landed at least half a metre further than Spiro's best throw.

As it hit the ground, a puff of dust was caught by the breeze. The dust seemed to spiral and dance across the field, as if it were celebrating Olly's success.

Eury smiled and patted Olly on the back. "Style and technique beat brute strength every time," he said.

"Especially with a little help from the spirit of the wind," said Olly, smiling.

He'd done it!

OLYMPIC FACTS!

DID YOU KNOW...?

The ancient Olympic Games began over 2,700 years ago in Olympia, in southwest Greece.

The ancient Games were held in honour of Zeus, king of the gods, and were staged every four years at Olympia.

In ancient times the discus was made from stone, wood, bronze or iron.

How far an athlete could hurl the discus was important, but competition judges also looked at the rhythm and style of the throw.

The ancient Olympics inspired the modern Olympic Games, which began in 1896 in Athens, Greece. Today, the modern Olympic Games are still held every four years in a different city around the world.

OLYMPIA

SHOO RAYNER